BIG TOP
SCOOBY-DOO!
JUNIOR NOVEL

Adapted by Kate Howard
Based upon the script written by Doug Langdale

SCHOLASTIC INC.

No part of this publication may be reproduced, stored in a
retrieval system, or transmitted in any form or by any means, electronic, mechanical,
photocopying, recording, or otherwise, without written permission of the publisher.
For information regarding permission, write to Scholastic Inc., Attention:
Permissions Department, 557 Broadway, New York, NY 10012.

ISBN 978-0-545-45717-0

12 11 10 9 8 7 6 5 4 3 2 1   12 13 14 15 16 17/0

Printed in the U.S.A.   40

Designed by Henry Ng
First printing, August 2012

PROLOGUE

Hidden under a cloak of darkness, a shadowy figure crept through a jewelry store. Nearby, a security guard slept soundly, unaware that a thief had sneaked past the locked front doors as he dozed and dreamed.

Without a word, the figure reached forward and lifted the top off a glass case. His hand stretched inside to touch the glowing ruby necklace that had been locked safely inside until just moments before. The intruder carefully lifted the necklace out of the case, and then slipped toward the door.

Suddenly, the store's alarms screamed. The guard was jolted awake. He fell out of his chair and then scrambled to his feet just in time to see the dark figure on his video monitor. He rushed into the store, ready to bust the burglar.

But when the guard saw the shadowy figure up close, he wished he was still dreaming. Because it was no ordinary thief stealing that ruby. . . .

The guard tried to scream, but he couldn't. "No . . ." he cried, wishing the monster standing in front of him would disappear. "No . . ." the guard whimpered again as the shadowy creature crept closer.

At last, the guard gathered the strength to flee. He shrieked as he dropped his flashlight and ran, ran, ran—straight into a support column. He was knocked out cold.

The shadowy figure stepped forward, reaching out one clawed hand to grab him. It was not the guard's lucky day.

But just in the nick of time, police sirens blared outside the store. The figure decided the wimpy security guard wasn't worth it. He left the guard curled in a heap and crashed out the store's side door. He raced down the street and disappeared around a corner just as several police cars roared up to the front door.

"Freeze!" shouted a police office, jumping out of his car. Like the security guard, he was *sure* that he was about to become a hero. But the thief just looked back and snarled, its horrible face scarier than anything the officer had ever seen.

Another officer leaped out of his car. Both officers gaped in shock, too stunned to fire their weapons. The figure darted away, still clutching the ruby necklace.

"Was that your mom?" the second police officer asked, glancing at his partner.

"Dude, shut up!" the first police officer said. He was still confused about what it was they had just seen.

The policemen looked at each other, and then ran after the thief. As they rounded a corner, both men were knocked to the ground. The thief had jumped out of the shadows!

After it leaped over the officers, the shadowy figure darted away again. It was just about to round a corner when one police officer shot at it.

"Did I hit it?" the officer asked, stunned. "I think I hit it."

But the thief didn't even slow down. It kept running as though it were unstoppable.

The other officer stood up, not even bothering to take out his gun. "I don't think it matters much, unless you've got silver bullets in that thing." He paused for a minute, thinking about the creature they'd just seen. "Also, you're right. It did kind of look like my mom."

As the officers stood helplessly outside the store, the shadowy figure dashed toward safety. It ran through the streets and finally stopped at the top of a rocky cliff overlooking a circus tent.

The full moon shone down on the figure that clutched at the ruby necklace. Its sinister yellow eyes shone in the moonlight. The figure tipped back its head and howled.

CHAPTER 1

"A whole week in Atlantic City!" Daphne said, bouncing happily in the front seat of the Mystery Machine. "This is gonna be the best vacation since Pismo Beach!"

"Like, didn't we get attacked by a demon clam in Pismo Beach?" Shaggy asked.

Daphne shrugged. "Okay, since Santa Fe, then."

"Isn't that where we were chased by those radioactive cactus monsters?" Shaggy said.

"Since . . . Washington, DC?" Daphne suggested weakly.

"Washington, Washington." Shaggy tried to think back to their trip to Washington, DC, but all he could think about was how hungry he was. "What happened in Washington, DC?"

"Rincoln Remorial," Scooby-Doo said.

"Oh, yeah," Shaggy said happily. "The Lincoln Memorial came to life and tried to stomp on Scooby." He glanced over at his best buddy.

Scooby had zipped on a fake beard and set a stovepipe hat over his ears. He made a spooky face and reached toward Shaggy, his arms out like a zombie. "Ror score rand *RAARRGH*!"

Shaggy jumped. "Zoinks!"

"Calm down, guys," Velma grumbled. She hated when Shaggy and Scooby got wild in the back of the van, especially when she had to sit next to them. "This is Atlantic City! The fun capital of the world! It's nothing but fun, fun, fun. Beaches and shows and—"

"Aaahhh!" Shaggy screamed. Startled, Scooby jumped into Shaggy's arms and quivered. Shaggy pointed out the window. "Look! Wûlfsmöóon!"

Fred, Daphne, Velma, and Scooby all looked out the window to see what Shaggy was so excited about. A huge picture of Wulfric Von Rydingsvard shone down at them from a billboard on the side of the road.

"My favorite band!" Shaggy cried happily as Scooby scooted off his lap. "Like, gang, we have to see them while we're here! Their lead singer, Wulfric, is so awesome! He does that one song that goes—"

Scooby covered his ears as Shaggy shrieked and shouted.

"You think that's cool, check *this* out!" Fred cried above the sounds of Shaggy's hollering. "Look! A circus!"

"Ooooh . . ." Shaggy said sarcastically. "The Brancusi Circus. Like, yay."

"I love the circus!" Fred reminded them. "You know how I took that Circus Arts class last summer."

"We know. . . ." Daphne, Velma, Shaggy, and Scooby all said together. They'd heard about Fred's circus camp a few too many times.

"I think I really could have mastered the trapeze if I hadn't broken all those bones. The trick," he explained, "is not to fall."

Shaggy rolled his eyes. "That's great, Fred,

but, like, not everyone loves the—"

"We gotta see it tonight!" Fred cried.

Velma shook her head. "Really, I think we'd rather—"

"My treat!" Fred hollered.

"Maybe some other—" Daphne tried.

"I insist!" Fred sighed happily. He was really excited about this.

"But we don't—" Shaggy whined.

"I'm glad that's settled," Fred said, steering the car down the road toward the Brancusi Circus tent. "You guys are gonna love it."

Slumping down in his seat, Shaggy said, "Hooray. The circus."

By the time Fred pulled the Mystery Machine up to the circus, the sky had grown dim. The parking lot was mostly empty. As they walked up to the ticket booth, Shaggy noticed a huge sign that said: BRANCUSI CIRCUS PRESENTS: CELESTIA. The name of the show, Celestia, didn't make him any more excited than he already wasn't.

"Well, look at that, they don't open until tomorrow night," Shaggy said. "Let's go!"

Fred stopped him as Shaggy turned to head back to the van. "Hang on. I want to see if there's anyone here."

"Wait, no! Like, they're closed!" Shaggy gestured toward the dark ticket booth. "I am *not* going into a dark circus!"

Fred ignored him and made his way toward the circus grounds. "The gate's open," he said cheerfully. "Let's just have a little look around."

Daphne and Velma followed Fred inside the fence, but Shaggy and Scooby weren't going anywhere. Until they realized they were alone, and then they trailed along behind the others.

"Okay," Shaggy said reluctantly. "But I am not *staying* in a dark circus!" He looked around as they walked into the circus grounds. "Look at this place! Even the *stuffed animals* are scary!"

Shaggy and Scooby peeked around at the circus stuff, noticing smaller tents, trailers, and containers for circus equipment. They strolled through the small circus town nervously. "Come on, guys," Shaggy whined. "On the creepy scale, this ranks higher than a graveyard!"

"Ran old graveyard!" Scooby agreed.

"Higher than an old graveyard *in a swamp.* On fire!"

But Fred didn't seem the least bit alarmed. "Hello?" he called out hopefully. "Anybody here?"

Shaggy and Scooby were so busy trying to keep an eye on everything at once that they began to wander off. "Guys . . ." Shaggy whispered, not realizing that everyone except Scooby had gone off in a different direction. "I have a really bad feeling about—"

Suddenly, Shaggy turned and came face-to-face with a horrifying clown. *"Ahhhh!"*

"Rahhhhh!" Scooby echoed.

After a few seconds, Shaggy and Scooby realized it was nothing but an old circus banner. They both sighed, relaxing a little. But their sighs turned to screams when they turned to look for the others and, instead, found themselves staring at a huge, scary *something.*

"Ahhhhh!" Shaggy cried again. "Like, *run,* Scoob!"

"Rahhhhh!" Scooby howled.

CHAPTER 2

Shaggy and Scooby didn't get far before they crashed into Fred, Daphne, and Velma. All five fell to the ground in a giant heap.

"*Oof!*" Fred cried, startled. He looked up just in time to see the same tall, silhouetted figure that had scared Shaggy. *Aahhh!*" he shrieked.

Daphne and Velma joined in the screaming. Scooby and Shaggy were still howling with fear.

The figure stepped into the light. The gang stopped screaming when they realized it wasn't anything spooky, but actually a very tall young man. His nose was hooked, like an eagle's, and he had long hair. "What are you doing here?" the man barked in an eastern European accent.

"I'm sorry," Fred said. He adjusted his ascot and stood up, embarrassed "The gate was open, and we just thought . . ."

The man looked concerned. "Open? But I'm sure I locked—" He broke off, his words interrupted by the sound of a wolf howling somewhere nearby. "He is here!" the man said nervously, gesturing for Fred and the gang to follow him. "Come. I'm Marius. We should stick together."

"But what . . .?" Velma began.

"Come!" Marius hurried silently among the tents, trailers, and cargo containers. It was obvious he knew exactly where he was going. "He will not elude me this time," Marius muttered quietly as they walked.

"Who?" Daphne whispered.

"The werewolf!" Marius whispered back.

Shaggy and Scooby gulped loudly. "The werewolf!"

"Yes," Marius said, still speaking softly. Shaggy and Scooby hoped he wasn't speaking quietly because the werewolf was close enough to hear them. "I think he is this way." Marius pointed in the direction they were walking.

Shaggy and Scooby both immediately started walking backward. Within seconds, they had broken out into an all-out run. "Like, let's get outta here, Scoob!" Shaggy cried.

"Rokay!" Scooby agreed, matching Shaggy's pace. They ran this way and that. Soon they were far from the others. They hoped that meant they were also far away from the werewolf!

"Look, Scoob," Shaggy said. He pointed to some cages. "What are—?" Shaggy peered between the bars of the cage. Suddenly, a creature leaped toward them. Shaggy shrieked and jumped back.

The creature looked at Shaggy, then it jumped and shrieked, too. It reminded Shaggy of . . . Shaggy. "Heh, it's a baboon," Shaggy said, grinning when he realized the creature was copying him. Shaggy struck a thoughtful pose, and the baboon mimicked him again.

Scooby giggled. He made a silly monkey face at the baboon, and laughed when the baboon made the face right back at him. He tried a few other faces, chuckling as the baboon copied him.

"Let me try!" Shaggy cried after a while. He teased the baboon with a bunch of silly faces, and then tried out a scary monster face. The baboon shrieked and hid in the corner of his cage.

"Sorry, baboon-dude!" Shaggy said kindly. "Didn't mean to scare . . . you. . . ?" Shaggy suddenly had the feeling that someone was standing behind them. He turned around slowly.

Sure enough, a figure that looked a lot like Marius was right there. Shaggy relaxed. "Oh, it's just you again!"

But then the shadowy figure stepped into the light. It wasn't Marius this time . . . It was a hairy, yellow-eyed werewolf!

Shaggy and Scooby zoomed away from the cages, running for their lives. They swerved and scrambled through the empty circus. When they saw Velma and the others, they ducked and cowered behind them, pointing and gasping.

"Werewolf!" Shaggy screamed.

Everyone turned to look in the direction Shaggy and Scooby had come from.

"There's nothing there," Daphne said.

Fred nodded. "Yeah, guys, there's nothing—" He turned back to Shaggy and Scooby just in time to see the werewolf creeping up behind Shaggy.

"Nothing?" Shaggy said. "That's a relief!" He noticed the look on Fred's face. "Like, it's right behind me, isn't it?"

The creature snarled, showing its vicious claws.

Fred, Daphne, and Marius hurried off in one direction as Velma, Shaggy, and Scooby raced away in the other.

A few minutes later, Shaggy slowed to a walk. "Like, I think we lost him."

"I think we lost everyone, Shaggy," Velma observed.

"All I know is I don't wanna see anything big and hairy," Shaggy said. He looked around, noticing a sign advertising a bearded lady. "Except maybe that." He grinned.

"This place sure is empty," Velma said. "Let's see if we can find that werewolf."

"Find it?" Shaggy said nervously. "I want to run away from it like a terrified schoolgirl!"

"Reah," Scooby agreed.

"Then let's find it so you know which way to run," Velma suggested. She stopped, bending over to examine something on the ground.

Shaggy looked at her like she was crazy. Then he walked on, saying, "That kinda makes sense." He looked around at signs and statues as they passed through the narrow passageways in the circus. "You know, Scoob, I think it went away."

"Ruh-uh!" Scooby said. "Rook!" The werewolf's shadow stretched toward them. It was back!

Scooby and Shaggy both turned and raced away. It wasn't until they'd put some serious distance between themselves and the wolf that they realized Velma was no longer with them.

"Velma!" Shaggy called. But the only answer was the call of a wolf, howling hungrily nearby.

A few moments later, Shaggy and Scooby found Marius, Daphne, and Fred. "Velma! She—"

"Quiet!" Marius said with a sneer. He was standing face-to-face with the werewolf! Marius held out a bunch of garlic. "Back!"

The werewolf took another step closer. Daphne leaned close to Marius and whispered, "That's vampires. Garlic—that scares away vampires."

"Are you sure?" Marius asked nervously.

As if in answer to his question, the werewolf reached forward and smacked the garlic from Marius's hand. Then it roared in his face.

"Pretty sure!" Daphne cried.

The werewolf lunged close again, prepared to attack. Just as Shaggy began to wonder how he would taste in werewolf stew, a brilliant light flashed on. Startled, the werewolf recoiled and fled across the tops of trailers.

Just as quickly as they'd gone on, the lights went off again. "I thought a little light might help," Velma said, emerging from behind a breaker box.

"Thank you," Marius said gratefully. "I didn't introduce myself properly before. I'm Marius Brancusi, the owner of this circus. How can I repay you?"

"Why don't you tell us what's going on here?" Velma said.

CHAPTER 3

"I inherited this circus from my uncle last year," Marius Brancusi began, pacing through his office. It was filled with circus posters and memorabilia—and some popcorn for Scooby and Shaggy. "The Brancusi Circus is world famous. It's an international circus, with acts from every country. I've been working to modernize it. I've been phasing out the animal acts, giving it more of a theatrical flair." He smiled proudly. "Also, I cleaned the toilets, which has been a huge improvement."

Marius pointed to the poster for the current circus show. "All of this has led to our latest show . . . Celestia!"

"This is so fantastic," Fred gushed. "Did I mention I love the circus?"

"Several times, yes," Marius said.

"But what about the werewolf?" asked Daphne.

Marius looked sad. "It's terrible. I thought tonight, while all my employees are having a night on the town, I might find some clues about the beast. I'm certain the werewolf must be someone who's part of the circus."

"You mean . . . in disguise?" Shaggy asked.

"Perhaps it's *not* a disguise." Marius looked even sadder. "It might be a real werewolf."

Shaggy gulped. "Like . . . zoinks!"

"You see, for the last few months, the creature has plagued us wherever we go. It's scared off many of my artists. And in every city we visit, it has stolen jewelry!"

"Rewelry?" Scooby asked.

Marius nodded. "Jewelry. It's very strange. Why would a werewolf want jewels?"

"Like, maybe he's a lady werewolf?" Shaggy said. The others stared at him like he was crazy.

"'Cause girls like pretty things?" They all continued to stare at him. "It was just a thought."

Velma suddenly looked excited. "I think I remember a case like this in eighteenth century Bavaria! May I use your computer?"

"Of course," Marius said, nodding.

"Yes, here it is . . . it was in Ingolstadt." Velma nodded, pointing to the computer screen. "A werewolf known as Hans collected certain gemstones and used them to increase his power. Normally a werewolf only becomes a wolf at the full moon. But with the right combination of jewels, Hans was able to change from man to wolf at any time. He and the werewolves he created terrorized Ingolstadt for decades."

"Werewolves he *created*?" Marius asked.

"Yes, anyone who is bitten by a werewolf and lives turns into a werewolf." Velma said this as though it were perfectly normal. "Apparently, the Ingolstadt werewolves claimed hundreds before being driven out by Maximillian the Third."

"Wow," Daphne said, looking at Scooby and Shaggy. "You guys are lucky you didn't get bitten."

Scooby and Shaggy were both thinking the same thing. "Yeah, like, we—" Shaggy gasped, and began to make choking sounds. He clutched at his throat desperately.

"Everyone get back!" Fred cried. "He's turning into a werewolf!"

Marius held his garlic up in front of his face again, warning Shaggy to stay back.

Shaggy looked around desperately as he choked. Finally, he punched himself in the stomach. A piece of popcorn flew from his mouth. "Some friends," Shaggy said, still gasping for air. "I need the Heimlich, and you're reaching for the silver bullets." He looked at Marius. "You get that? Silver bullets for werewolves, garlic for vampires."

Marius just stared at him. "Who are you? How do you know so much about werewolves?"

"We solve mysteries. It's kind of a hobby," Daphne explained.

"A hobby?" Marius said. "Stamp collecting is a hobby. Solving mysteries is—wait! Maybe you could help me investigate this werewolf!"

Fred squealed happily. "Yes! That's a great

idea! We could pose as circus performers!"

Daphne gave him a funny look. Then she turned to Marius with a nod. "Sure, why not?"

"Of course, it will be very dangerous. . . ." Marius said, thinking.

"And there's the why not," Shaggy said. "See ya!" He turned to go, with Scooby at his heels.

"We have to do it, Shaggy," Fred said.

Shaggy and Scooby just started walking, pushing Fred backward.

"For the good of the circus!" Fred begged.

"Forget it!" Shaggy said.

"For the safety of the public!" Fred cried.

"No way," Shaggy said, pushing Fred aside.

"For all the cotton candy you can eat!" Fred coaxed.

"Count me ou—" Shaggy began, and then stopped to think about it. "And churros?"

Fred nodded. "And churros."

"Like, dude, I'm in!" Shaggy said gleefully.

"Reah! Re, roo! Reah! Reah!" said Scooby.

"Well," Marius said, "if you're going to pass for circus artists, it's going to take a little work. . . ."

CHAPTER
4

Half an hour later, the gang gathered in the center of the big top. Marius had found them all costumes.

"So," Marius said, looking at the gang anxiously. "Do any of you have any circus skills?"

Fred's hand shot up. "I do! I took a Circus Arts class last summer!"

"Why am I not surprised?" Marius muttered. He looked at Fred, doubtful. "And what did you learn in this class?"

"Well," Fred said proudly, "I worked out on the trapeze a bit." He puffed out his chest, and then let it fall again. "But I ended up breaking a lot of bones."

"You seem to have healed well," Marius observed.

"What?" Fred asked, confused. "Oh! Not *my* bones. See, I was supposed to catch this guy and . . . well, I dropped him." He paused. "On to someone." He smiled sheepishly. "And they both fell into some other people."

Marius gasped. "That's terr—"

Fred cut him off. "Who hit the tent support, which tipped the popcorn cart, which set fire to the audience risers, which collapsed with forty-eight people sitting on them."

Marius cleared his throat, as Fred looked at the floor. "Well, I'm sure it wasn't your fault."

"No, it was. But I did learn a valuable lesson about the trapeze."

"Which was?" Marius asked.

"Don't drop people," Fred said confidently. "Oh, and don't fall."

"Yes, those are kind of the basics." Marius looked thoughtful. "How would you like a junior second-assistant backup trapeze position?"

Fred saluted Marius enthusiastically. "It would be an honor, sir!"

"You are a strange fellow," Marius mused, "but I admire your neckwear." He looked at the others, who were still gathered around awkwardly. "Anyone else have any talents they might apply?"

Daphne glanced around before saying, "When I was a kid I used to do a little motorcycle act."

"Really?" Marius said doubtfully. "It takes years of practice to—"

As Marius spoke, Daphne noticed a fancy motorcycle parked in the center of the ring. "It went like this," she called, hopping on the motorcycle. The rest of the gang watched as Daphne drove the bike up a ramp, through a hoop, and along a narrow cable. As a finishing touch, she guided the motorcycle around an upside-down loop and skidded to a stop an inch from Marius.

"Right," he said, impressed. "That will do."

Marius turned to Shaggy, Scooby, and Velma. Velma scooted behind Scooby, trying to hide. She was much more comfortable solving mysteries in her favorite skirt and turtleneck.

"Unfortunately," Marius said, looking at Scooby, "I've phased animal acts out of my circus, but I could make an exception." He looked at Shaggy and said, "Your friend here seems very well trained."

Scooby was sure Marius was talking to him. He smiled at Shaggy, and then patted him on the back. "Roh, he is. Shake, Shaggy."

Shaggy shook Scooby's hand.

"Reg."

"Like, please, please, please!" Shaggy said.

Scooby gave Shaggy a Scooby Snack and ruffled his hair. "Rood boy!"

Marius looked confused. "Uh, just for the sake of tradition, maybe you"—he pointed to Scooby, who was still patting Shaggy on the head like a good dog—"maybe *you* should do the tricks."

Shaggy nodded. "That's probably a good idea, 'cause, like, Scooby does more circus-y stuff than me. Show him, Scoob!"

Scooby hopped up on a giant ball and danced

around on it, and then juggled a bunch of stars in the air before he finally somersaulted backward toward the others. "Ra-daaaa!" he cried.

Marius looked at Shaggy and said, "You've taught him all this?"

Shaggy pouted and said, "Like, Scoob *tried* to teach me all this, but I just can't get it."

Scooby patted Shaggy's back comfortingly.

"And you . . ." Marius looked at Velma, who was hiding behind a giant post. "Hello?"

"Hi," Velma said, peeking out at him nervously.

"If you're afraid, I could put you on the churro cart," Marius suggested.

"No, no! I can do it." Velma tried to sound confident.

"Do what?"

Velma shrugged. "I don't know. Something."

Marius looked at a list. "There are still a few acts I could use. How about knife throwing?"

"No."

"Sword-swallowing?" Marius suggested.

"No."

"Fire eating?"

"No!" Velma's eyes grew wider.

"Bullet catching?"

"NO!"

"Hmm," Marius said thoughtfully. "The only thing that's left is . . . the Human Comet."

"That doesn't sound so bad," Velma muttered.

"You get shot out of a cannon," Marius said.

Velma looked like she was going to be sick. "Uh . . ."

"Oh, look," Marius said, suddenly distracted by the sound of cars outside the tent. "The rest of my performers are starting to get back from town. I have to get everyone prepared." He hustled the gang out of the circus tent. "Meet me here in the morning."

"What time?" Shaggy asked with a yawn.

"Five o'clock," Marius said.

Shaggy snorted. "There is no five o'clock in the *morning*!" He laughed at the idea of getting up that early. Then he looked at his friends, and no one else was laughing. "Like, is there?"

Scooby shook his head. "Ri have a bad reeling about ris. . . ."

CHAPTER 5

The next morning, the Mystery, Inc. gang dragged themselves back to the circus tent at the crack of dawn. Everyone was yawning, except Fred, who was ready for his big day on the trapeze.

Shaggy was still half-asleep as they ambled up toward the big top. He kept falling behind the others. He would never have made it out of bed if Scooby hadn't grabbed his shirt in his mouth and dragged him along like a toy.

"I wonder if we should use code names while we're undercover?" Fred suggested as they approached the door of the tent.

"Ro . . ." Scooby said, shoving Shaggy from behind to keep him upright.

"No," Velma seconded.

"No . . ." Daphne said, yawning.

Fred ignored them. He was getting excited about his idea. "I could be Dominic St. Chinard, ne'er-do-well son of a New England shipping magnate who—"

"No!" Scooby, Velma, and Daphne said again.

"Finally, you're here!" Marius said, stepping out from behind the concessions stand. "Come on! You have to meet your fellow circus artists . . ."

"Yay!" Fred cried happily.

Marius looked at him strangely. "Remember, any one of them could be a bloodthirsty monster."

"Boo!" Scooby said.

"Come along," Marius said, waving the gang toward the animal cages. "Meet Whitney Doubleday. He's our animal trainer."

"Ruh?" Scooby asked, looking around and seeing no one. But Marius was already gone, as were Velma, Daphne, and Fred. He and Shaggy were alone in the animal tents. "Rhere is Whitney Doubleray? Rello?"

"Yes?" A door swung open, and there was

Fred, Daphne, Velma, Shaggy, and Scooby-Doo are on vacation in Atlantic City. They decide to check out the local circus.

It's only a matter of time before the gang finds themselves in the middle of a mystery! Marius, the circus owner, tells them about a werewolf that's been haunting his troupe.

Before they know it, the werewolf finds Scooby and Shaggy!

Velma does a little research and learns about a werewolf seeking jewels to increase its power.

OLIVERIO
THE TRAPEZE ARTIST

ARCHAMBAULT
THE STRONG MAN

The gang decides to go undercover to find out if the werewolf is a circus troupe member in disguise!

DOUBLEDAY
THE ANIMAL TRAINER

SCHMATKO
THE CLOWN

It's showtime! But — *ruh-roh!* — the werewolf and its pals attack in the middle of the performance!

It's Scooby-Doo and Shaggy to the rescue!

The gang gets a special thank-you from Shaggy's favorite band. *Scooby-Dooby-Doo!*

Whitney Doubleday . . . hanging upside down.

"Ragh!" Scooby cried in alarm.

Shaggy had drifted off to sleep again. His eyes peeked open for just a moment, and then closed again. "Wha' happen . . . Scoob?" He snorted and went back to his dream.

"Oh, terribly sorry to startle you," Doubleday said, lowering himself to the ground. Doubleday was a fit, middle-aged man. When he got a closer look, Scooby could see that the animal trainer had been hanging upside down from a bar—for no obvious reason. "Thirty minutes every day," Doubleday explained. "Marvelous for the lower back." He thrust out his hand to shake. "Whitney Doubleday, animal trainer."

Scooby shook his hand.

"Good boy," Doubleday said, offering Scooby a treat.

Shaggy, who'd heard the sound of tasty crunching, peeked open an eye. "Whuzuh?" He shook Doubleday's hand sleepily.

"Good boy," Doubleday said, offering Shaggy a treat. Then he laughed and said, "Sorry, after forty years of handing out treats to animals, it's become a habit. . . ."

Shaggy nodded, chewing his treat happily. "Thanks," he said, finally waking up. "I'm, uh, Shaggy Rogers. Also an animal trainer . . ."

Scooby looked at him, obviously annoyed.

"Well, like, I guess I'm more of an animal . . . partner." Scooby began to smile. "Uh, animal *buddy*."

Scooby grinned and put his arm around Shaggy. "Reah, rartners. Buddy! Ree-hee-hee."

"Well," said Doubleday, studying Shaggy and Scooby. "I suppose if you're a team, that's different. I thought it was odd that Marius hired you. See, he eliminated all the trained animals from the circus."

Shaggy realized this was his chance to gather clues. That was what they were supposed to be doing, after all. As they strolled among the cages, admiring a lion, a bear, an elephant, and four baboons, Shaggy said, "Really? Well, you must be angry and bitter, and seeking revenge if he got rid of the animal acts."

Doubleday laughed. "Not at all! I was retiring anyway. The public doesn't want trained animals anymore. Too many stories about abusive training techniques. Of course, *I* never hurt any of my animals. Right, Leoni?"

The lion looked at Doubleday and roared.

Doubleday smiled and continued. "But there are a few bad apples out there. No, I'm afraid my kind of act is a thing of the past."

Shaggy nodded. "So, um, have you ever trained, oh, I don't know . . ." He was trying to figure out a way to be sneaky with his questions, but he was too tired to be clever. Finally, he said, "For instance, just off the top of my head, have you ever trained, uh . . . wolves?"

Doubleday shook his head. "Wolves? No. No one works with wolves. They're too unpredictable. I'd have better luck trying to train a hurricane."

"Oh," Shaggy said, disappointed. He'd been hoping to solve the mystery right then and there. "So . . . if you're not in the show, why are you and your animals here?"

"We're just along for the ride," Doubleday

said. "I'm transporting the animals to a sanctuary in California." He stopped walking when they got to the baboon cage. "I think I'll miss my baboons the most. So much like people, don't you think?"

Shaggy shrugged. "I don't really see any resemblance."

"*Escucheme!*" Doubleday barked loudly, obviously talking to the baboons. "*Bailadores!*"

Much to Shaggy and Scooby's surprise, the baboons began to waltz in pairs.

"*Soldados!*" Doubleday cried, showing off for his new audience.

The baboons snapped to attention like soldiers.

"*Boxeadores!*"

The baboons pretended to box with one another.

"*Descanso!*"

The baboons relaxed again, and went back to picking at their fur. Doubleday looked proud. "I always use Spanish commands," he explained.

"The animals are less likely to hear shouts from the audience and get confused. *Inclinarse!*" Doubleday said.

The baboons took a bow.

Shaggy and Scooby clapped wildly.

"Wow, Scoob!" Shaggy said. "You think we could do something like that?"

"Rure!" Scooby said. *"Railador!"*

Shaggy began to waltz with Scooby. Doubleday shook his head. He wasn't sure if he should be impressed. "Well, it's unusual; I'll give them that. . . ."

Meanwhile, on the other side of the circus, Fred, Daphne, and Velma were finding out more about their new circus jobs. "Velma," Marius said, pointing to a huge, hulking, hairy beast of a man, "meet Archambault, our strongman. You'll be working with him."

Velma backed away nervously. "Uhhh. . . ."

Archambault smiled at Velma. "Don't be afraid; big hairy man is not werewolf," he said. Velma wasn't so sure. "You heard about werewolf? Terrible, terrible. Very bad for circus, *oui*?"

Velma continued to back away.

"Okay!" said Archambault. He knelt down in front of Velma and put his hand on the ground, palm up.

"Um, what are you—?" Velma said. She was wondering if she should have just offered to man the churro stand.

"Ah! Archambault forget; you are new to the circus. Please, you should step on the hand."

"What?!"

"Step on the hand! Trust Archambault." Archambault smiled, and Velma reluctantly put her foot on his huge palm. He lifted her up like she weighed nothing and strolled along with her standing on the palm of his hand.

"Whoa!" Velma cried.

"Archambault is not fake like some strong

mans, see? Archambault is genuine article! Strongest man in Quebec, eh?"

"But why—?" Velma looked down at the ground.

"Is part of act! I carry you to cannon," Archambault explained. "Then you climb in, I pull lever, boom-boom, land in net. *Oui?*"

Velma nodded. "Um, I guess?"

"Good. We do some practicings. Make sure you shouldn't break head." Archambault tapped gently on Velma's head, and then shoved her into the cannon. "Human comet . . . fire!" A burst of smoke popped out of the cannon, along with Velma's costume.

Velma poked her head out of the cannon. "Sorry," she said, straightening her hair and glasses. "I think I tensed up."

Daphne watched Velma peek out of the human cannon from across the main ring. Marius had left Velma with Archambault while he took Fred to the trapeze area.

"Those are the people I'll be performing with?" Fred asked, looking up at the aerial team.

"Not performing!" Marius reminded him. "You're junior second-assistant backup trapeze. That means you stand by the net and do as little as possible. If someone falls, you help them out of the net. Oliverio! Lena! This is Fred."

Fred waved as Marius leaned over to say, "By the way . . . Oliverio is very jealous, so don't look at Lena. But don't *look* like you're not looking at her, because that makes her flirty."

Fred looked confused. "Wait. What?"

Marius didn't answer. He just led Daphne away.

As Oliverio and Lena drew closer to Fred, Fred grew more and more nervous. He looked away from Lena, then at her, and then straight up at nothing at all. He wasn't sure exactly *where* to look, and his head wobbled and danced all around.

"Ah," Oliverio said, studying Fred carefully.

"The new net boy. Something is wrong with your neck?"

"No," Fred said, still looking all around— trying to both *look* and *not* look at Lena. He grew more confused by the second.

"Maybe his cute little scarf is too tight," Lena said flirtatiously. "I loosen it for you, *ja*?" She pranced off, leaving Fred to stare after her.

As she sashayed away, Oliverio shot Fred a look that could kill. "Net Boy, you stay away from Lena or I pop you head off like the bottle cap."

Fred scratched his head as Oliverio stormed away. "Nice to meet you, too. I'm Fred."

Outside the big top, Marius led Daphne toward the clown trailer. "Clowns are fun!" she exclaimed, following Marius.

"Fun like head lice," Marius muttered, then turned to go. "Got to go! They're right in there. . . ."

Daphne peeked into the clown trailer. A

sad-faced clown was applying his makeup. He was dressed in a red and purple costume covered with stars and moons. "Um, hello?" Daphne said.

The clown grumbled. "Maybe I don't feel like hello."

Daphne stepped inside the trailer. "Are you one of the clowns?"

"No! I'm an actor! I have merely undertaken the role of a clown." The clown stared her down. "*That* is a clown." He pointed.

Daphne looked at where the clown was pointing. All she saw was a pile of old rags. Then a head popped out of the rags, and the pile stood up. It was another clown. He honked a horn, making Daphne laugh. "Hello! I'm Daphne Blake."

"Yes," the first clown said, studying Daphne. "The motorcycle girl. Marius told us about you. This"—the grouchy clown pointed to the clown that had been posing as a pile of rags—"this buffoon here is Sisko."

"Pleased to meet you!" Daphne said.

"And I . . . am Shmatko!"

"Shmatko! What a great clown name!" Daphne said.

Shmatko stomped angrily. "It is NOT a clown name! I am Svyatopolk Stanislavevich Shmatko! Sisko—*that* is a clown name. Shmatko is a name of great dignity! Once I toured the Soviet Union performing the classics. Chekov! Pushkin! Turgenev!"

"Bulgakov?" Daphne said helpfully.

"You know Bulgakov?" Shmatko asked. He looked delighted. "At last, a person of culture! I like this motorcycle girl."

Sisko honked in agreement.

"Okay," Shmatko said happily. "I go make smoothie. Who wants smoothie? One strawberry for Sisko . . ." Sisko honked in agreement. "Motorcycle Girl?"

Daphne shook her head. "Oh, no thanks."

"Fine, suit yourself. Back in a littles." Shmatko skipped happily out of the trailer.

As he hurried away, a shadowy figure followed him, its red eyes glowing. Shmatko turned a corner just as a clawed hand reached for him. . . .

CHAPTER 6

A few hours later, the gang gathered in Marius's office.

"So," Fred said. "The circus is a little different than I'd imagined."

"How so?" Marius asked.

"It's fully of crazy people! Oliverio threatened to pop my head off!"

Daphne nodded. "Marius, I don't know if your werewolf is real or not, but if you're looking for someone with a grudge against the circus, there are plenty of suspects."

"Like, that Doubleday guy says he doesn't mind losing his job, but I don't know about that. . . ." Shaggy said thoughtfully.

"And Shmatko has a lot of bitterness about being a clown," Daphne added.

Velma said, "Archambault *seems* nice, but he sure *looks* like a werewolf!"

"I know, I know," Marius said, sighing. "And there's one more suspect. . . ." He held up a Wûlfsmöóon poster. It showed a huge picture of Wulfric Von Rydingsvard rocking out.

"Wûlfsmöóon?!" Shaggy said, gaping at the picture of his favorite band. "Like, no way!"

"They've performed in every town where the werewolf has appeared," Marius said sadly.

"Actually," Shaggy said thoughtfully, "their lead singer *does* say he's a werewolf." He laughed. "But he also says he's from Sweden."

"And he isn't?" Fred asked.

"Duh," Shaggy answered, laughing. "Sweden's just a made-up place, like fairyland or Australia. I bet you think kangaroos are real, too!"

Fred looked at the others. "Uh, Shaggy . . ."

Shaggy and Scooby both giggled. "Sweden!" Shaggy said, wiping his eyes. "Duh . . ."

"Rangaroos!" Scooby chuckled.

Marius stared at Shaggy. "Has he been kicked in the head or something?"

Fred shook his head. "Not yet."

"Like, all this speculationing is making me hungry, Scoob," Shaggy said. Scooby nodded and licked his lips. "Guys, we are heading for the legendary Cap'n Fatty's Rib Ranch, home of the more-than-all-you-can-eat special. You eat as much as you can, and then they force dessert down your throat with a spatula!"

"Rum, rum!" Scooby said.

"Anyone care to join us?" Shaggy offered.

Daphne looked disgusted. "We'll catch up with you."

Shaggy and Scooby strolled out of the circus and toward town. "Scoob, after this we'll have visited almost all of the greatest rib joints in America," Shaggy said, rubbing his stomach.

"Reah!"

"All that's left is that one where the ribs come with a coupon for free heart surgery. What's it called?"

"Rhe Rib Reaper," Scooby said.

"Yeah, the Rib Reaper. Some day, Scooby-Doo, some . . ." Shaggy's voice trailed off as the sound of footsteps echoed behind them. Shaggy and Scooby swiveled around to look behind them.

In the shadows, just a few steps behind, red eyes glowed back at them. Something growled. It wasn't Shaggy's stomach.

Shaggy stared at the beast and said, quietly, "Okay, Scoob . . . when I say *run*, I want you to—"

Scooby ran as fast as his feet would go.

"I didn't say *run* yet!" Shaggy called, chasing after him.

Shaggy and Scooby raced into an old museum. Under ordinary circumstances, neither of them would have dared to venture inside a creepy old museum at night, in the dark. But when they had to choose between that and a growling werewolf, their decision was obvious.

The two buddies dashed through the front doors. They were in such a hurry that they failed to notice that the door had already been ripped off its hinges. As they plowed through the front hallway, they tripped over something—and the *something* groaned.

"Aghhhh!" Scooby and Shaggy screamed, realizing there was a security guard lying in a heap on the floor. The sound of breaking glass made them jump up and look around. That's when they noticed a werewolf reaching into a smashed glass case. The werewolf snatched up an emerald necklace. Then it turned and pounced at Scooby and Shaggy.

Scooby and Shaggy were on the run again. They sprinted out the museum door, down the front steps, and back into the street.

"Like, how did that werewolf get in there so fast? One minute it was out in the street with us, then the next it was . . ." Shaggy trailed off.

Scooby shrugged. "Ri ron't row!"

The werewolf was gaining on them.

"Like, run again, Scoob!" Shaggy cried. He and Scooby sped across the street. As they dashed and darted, the Mystery Machine came swerving around the corner. The van drove right up onto the sidewalk, knocking into some garbage cans. The cans crashed down on top of the werewolf.

Fred, Daphne, and Velma jumped out of the van. "Shaggy! Scooby! What's going on?"

"Werewolf!" Shaggy gasped, pointing to a werewolf that was between the gang and the van.

Fred, Daphne, Velma, Shaggy, and Scooby stared at the werewolf. It was dressed in ripped red and purple clothes, with a vicious snarl on its face. They backed away as it drew closer. That was when they heard a second growl behind them.

"There's two of them!" Fred cried. The second werewolf was holding the stolen jewels in its gnarled fist.

"And that one . . ." Daphne said, staring at the first werewolf. "I think it's Shmatko the clown!" She held out her hands to the werewolf in purple and red. "Shmatko, it's *me*. Motorcycle Girl!"

The werewolf snapped at her.

"He doesn't seem very friendly," Fred noted.

"Well, he wasn't all that friendly *before* he turned into a werewolf," Daphne said with a shrug.

The werewolves were closing in. Frightened,

the gang ran. As they zoomed past a fruit stand, Fred kicked one of the shelves free. Apples spilled everywhere, tripping the werewolves and giving the gang a few extra seconds to escape.

"This way!" Daphne cried, pulling Velma along behind her.

"No, this way!" Fred called, dragging Scooby and Shaggy.

When the werewolves finally scrambled to their feet again, they caught sight of Velma and Daphne first. The girls were peeking around a corner, trying to hide.

"Uh-oh," Daphne muttered. She and Velma ran again, squeezing between some bags of trash down a dark alley.

"Over here!" Velma yelled. She pointed to a manhole on the street below them. Daphne pried up the cover and they both scurried inside. But the werewolves spotted them! They reached their horrible claws out to pull the lid off.

A screeching noise stopped them just in the nick of time. The Mystery Machine was charging toward the werewolves . . . and it was pushing a huge dumpster full of garbage!

"It's time to take out the trash!" Fred cried from behind the wheel.

The werewolves leaped away from the manhole and skittered up the side of a building. From the roof, they looked down at Fred, Shaggy, and Scooby, and howled.

"Dang," Fred moaned, climbing out of the Mystery Machine. "They're fast."

"Rikes! Rhut's rhat?" Scooby yelped, startled by a loud banging sound from below.

Shaggy sighed. "I'm gonna guess it's Daphne and Velma, pounding on the manhole cover that we just buried under a ton of garbage."

"We're in the sewer!" Velma yelled.

"Get us outta here!" Daphne whined.

Fred, Shaggy, and Scooby looked at the huge pile of garbage and groaned.

"Well," Fred said reluctantly, "I guess we better start digging. . . ."

CHAPTER
7

After Daphne and Velma had been dug out of the trash, the gang returned to the circus. They rushed into Marius's office, ready to tell him all about their encounter with the werewolves.

"Thank goodness you're here!" Marius cried, as soon as he saw them. "Shmatko's missing! Sisko hasn't seen him since early this morning."

From the corner of Marius's office, Sisko honked sadly.

Daphne glanced at Sisko. Then she said, "He's a werewolf."

"What?!" Marius shouted.

Sisko honked in alarm.

"We just got chased by *two* werewolves,"

Daphne replied. "And one was wearing Shmatko's clothes."

Shaggy nodded. "They broke into a museum and stole an emerald necklace."

"He's collecting jewels," Velma said. "And he's making more werewolves! It's just like in Ingolstadt!"

Marius shook his head. "I know this is bad, but we've got a show to do in half an hour!"

Sisko honk-honked in response.

"Nothing is impossible, Sisko! Daphne, you'll stand in for Shmatko," Marius declared.

"I'm doing what now?" Daphne asked.

"We'll need to fill some time. Fred, can you walk a tightrope?" Marius looked worried.

"Of course I maybe can!" Fred said happily.

Archambault popped into the office just in time to hear the discussion. "And Archambault can do cowboy routine!" He was wearing a cowboy costume that looked especially strange on his huge body.

"Not the cowboy routine . . ." Marius grumbled.

Archambault pouted. "Why you no like

cowboy routine? Is best superb! I can make it space cowboy for this 'Celestia' thing."

"Fine, do it," Marius sighed. "Come on everyone." He waved everyone out of his office. "Get into costume. It's showtime, folks!" He paused, sniffing at the air. "What is that *smell*?"

Velma pointed to Daphne. "We were in the sewer. . . ."

"And we were digging through garbage," Fred said, pointing to Shaggy and Scooby.

Archambault doubled over with laughter. "You Americans really know how to party!"

A short while later, everyone was dressed and ready for that night's circus. Velma twitched nervously in her Human Comet outfit, and Daphne looked uncomfortable in her clown getup.

"Everyone ready?" Marius asked, rubbing his hands together.

"No!" Daphne and Velma both cried.

"Great," Marius said, heading out toward the center of the big top. "I'm going to start the show."

Within seconds, fog began filling the performance ring, and music blared through the speakers. Marius leaped out of the fog and strode to the center of the ring. "Ladies and gentlemen! With the finest talent from five continents, the Brancusi Circus presents . . . Celestia!"

The audience cheered madly. The show was underway.

Archambault was up first, stuffed into the cowboy outfit he'd paired with a space helmet. "Yippee-ki-yay, I am the space cowboy, *oui*? But in Quebec, cowboy don't do things the easy way, ha-ha!" He reached over and lifted a horse off the ground. The audience stared at him as he trotted around the ring, carrying a horse.

"See what I mean?" Marius whispered to Fred in the wings. "His cowboy act makes people uncomfortable."

"Totally," Fred muttered.

Luckily, things improved from there. Fred

was a hit on the trapeze, and Daphne turned out to be a much better clown than she would ever have imagined.

Finally, Marius stepped out into the ring to say, "Ladies and gentlemen, may I present . . . Scooby and Shaggy!"

The audience applauded as Shaggy and Scooby paraded out of the fog.

"Hello, Atlantic City!" Shaggy cried, waving to everyone wildly. "I give you . . . Scooby-Doo!"

Scooby took a bow. Then he began his act. He juggled, he danced, he spun plates, and he rode a giant unicycle upside down and backward. When no one thought it could possibly get any more amazing, Scooby began his real show: fire eating, throwing knives, and a dozen other tricks that no one had ever seen before.

"Ra daaaa!" he cheered at the end. He was barely even out of breath.

The crowd went wild.

Shaggy looked at Scooby and grinned. "Thank you, thank you!" he shouted at the audience. "I'm Shaggy, his, uh . . . trainer!"

Somehow, the crowd got even louder then. "Shag-gy! Shag-gy! Shag-gy!"

Scooby looked at Shaggy, and then pointed to himself. "Rhut rabout re?"

Shaggy just soaked up the cheers.

"That went well," Marius called as they bowed and stepped out of the main ring.

Now it was Velma's turn. "You're up, Human Comet!" Marius told her.

Velma shook with nerves. "I can't do this!"

"Don't worry," Archambault reassured her as he carried her toward the cannon. "You're going to be fine."

"You think so?" Velma asked.

"Eh." Archambault shrugged. "Fifty-fifty."

But before Velma could be shot through the air, a scream tore through the big top. "Werewolves!" a woman in the audience shrieked. "Werrrrrewolves!"

Everyone turned in time to see two were-wolves dash across the center of the main ring. The audience began to applaud. "Those costumes are awesome!" someone yelled.

Shaggy and Scooby peeked out to see what was going on. The werewolves that had chased them out of the museum were now snarling and snapping and running through the circus.

The audience laughed. "Werewolves! What a great idea!" they called. Everyone thought the werewolves were just actors in the circus!

"Everybody out!" Marius called out to the audience. "Follow the ushers. Please evacuate in an orderly fashion!"

The crowd still believed the werewolves were just part of the act. They cheered and clapped as they left the big top.

"Aahhh!" Shaggy yelped as the werewolves drew closer to him and Scooby. "Like, don't bite us! I don't wanna be a werewolf!"

"Ri'm ralready a dog!" Scooby whimpered. He and Shaggy hopped onto Daphne's motorcycle, trying to outrun the werewolves.

"Get away. Shoo!" Shaggy snapped at the werewolves. "Go chase a cat."

The motorcycle tipped as Shaggy and Scooby zoomed awkwardly around the big top with the werewolves right behind them. *Ahh!* No bitey!" Shaggy scolded. "Like, I am not a chew toy!"

"There has to be something we can do," Marius said helplessly.

Fred thought for a moment. "Usually I drop a net on—" He looked up and saw the trapeze act's safety net. "Ooh, that's a big net! Shaggy! Scooby! Lead them over this way!"

"I'll try," Shaggy yelled, shaking his leg at the werewolf. Scooby's arms were wrapped around Shaggy's head, blocking his view. When he realized his buddy couldn't see, Scooby reached his feet around Shaggy and steered the bike toward Fred.

"Now!" Fred yelled to Marius. They pulled at the ropes on either side of the safety net and it dropped on the two werewolves. "Got 'em!"

Everyone ran over and began to dig through the piles of netting—even Sisko, Oliverio, and Lena. "Come on," Marius said as they dug through the trap. "They have to be here."

But when they got to the bottom of the pile, it was obvious that the trap had failed.

"How could they just disappear like that?" Doubleday asked, appearing out of nowhere to help with the search.

Sisko honked twenty-six times.

"Maybe . . ." Doubleday said. He obviously understood what Sisko had been trying to say. "But where would they hide the forklift?"

Velma paced near Marius. She was still trying to figure out why the werewolves had attacked during the circus. "Why did they attack now? They weren't stealing jewels. They went right for Scooby and Shaggy. . . ."

"You think they were trying to scare us off?" Fred asked.

But before anyone could answer, Shaggy and Scooby zipped by on the motorcycle. "How do you, like, stop this thing?!" Shaggy cried as they sped into the wings.

Daphne winced as a loud crash echoed through the big top. The motorcycle's motor came to a sudden stop. "That's one way. . . ."

CHAPTER

8

That night, everyone slept in Marius's office, just in case the werewolf came back. They woke with a start the next morning when Marius hollered, "Unbelievable!"

Fred, Daphne, Shaggy, Scooby, and Velma all leaped up. Scooby jumped into Shaggy's arms for protection. What's that?! Is it the werewolves?"

Marius was smiling broadly. "There were critics in the audience last night!" He slapped down a pile of newspapers on this desk.

"Circus critics?" Velma asked.

Marius nodded. "These are the most incredible reviews I've ever seen! They all assumed the werewolves were part of the show. And look at this!" He pointed to the front page. Everyone crowded around him and saw Shaggy grinning back at them. Scooby was in the very bottom corner of the picture. "They're calling Shaggy the greatest circus artist since Felix Adler!"

Scooby unwrapped his arms from Shaggy's neck. "Rhut?!"

Shaggy's face reddened, and he couldn't stop smiling. "I'm so excited . . . and I would be so much more excited if I had any idea who Felix Adler was!"

"This is great, Shaggy," Daphne said, patting him on the back.

"Congratulations!" Fred seconded.

Velma nodded. "Way to go!"

Scooby looked disappointed. "Rhut rabout re?"

"Well," Marius said, trying to come up with something. "Listen to this: 'The performance young Shaggy Rogers gets from his trained dog, Scabby —'"

"Rabby?!" Scooby barked.

"— is so remarkable that one might almost

believe the animal has a mind of its own!'" Marius continued.

Scooby snatched the newspaper away from Marius. "Ri *do* have a rind of ri own!"

"It's true," Daphne said. "He does."

Marius didn't really seem to care. "Well, this is fantastic news! Excuse me, I have to show these around." He hurried out of his office to share the reviews with the other members of the circus.

"Looks like we're a hit, huh?" Shaggy said, beaming at Scooby.

"'Rabby . . .'" Scooby moaned.

As Shaggy reveled in his newfound fame, Archambault burst into Marius's trailer. "You have heard? The newsies are loving the show! We sell many tickets now, *oui*?" He looked around on the shelves, searching for something. "You all be sure to come to breakfast today, okay? Archambault is going to make his famous crêpes!" He held up a key. "Aha! Kitchen trailer key. Breakfast be ready soon."

As Archambault backed away from the shelf, he knocked a book to the floor. It landed at Velma's feet.

"What . . . ?" she asked, picking it up. It looked very old. "This is a book about the Ingolstadt were-wolves!" she cried.

Archambault and the others stared at her.

"But I thought Marius had never heard of them!" Daphne said, peering over Velma's shoulder.

"That's what he *said*. . . ." Fred mused.

Shaggy rubbed his chin scruff. "Like, maybe he just bought that book yesterday?"

Velma continued to look through the old book. "It was printed in Estonia in eighteen fifty-three. You really think Marius could have found this in just a day?"

"What are you saying?" Archambault asked. "That Marius is werewolf?"

Fred didn't look convinced. "But last night, he was with us when the werewolves attacked."

"He still might be one of them," Daphne said slowly. "Maybe he can change whenever he wants, like in Ingolstadt."

Velma pointed to something in the book. "Someone has circled all the jewels that Hans supposedly collected. They're the same ones our werewolf has stolen . . . except one." She held up the book. Someone had circled an illustration of a large, black gem. "It says it's a 'carbonado.'"

"What's a . . . car now?" Shaggy asked.

Archambault shrugged. "Carbonado . . . very puzzlement, *oui*? Okay! Time to make the crêpes. Breakfast in one hour!" He headed out toward the kitchen.

Shaggy's stomach growled. "Ooh, I'm not gonna last an hour. Hey, Scoob, is Cap'n Fatty's Rib Ranch open for breakfast?"

"Reah!" Scooby cried.

"Then let's head on out, *Scabby*!" Shaggy laughed all the way to the restaurant, but Scooby got more and more annoyed by the minute.

While Shaggy and Scooby were at the diner, Velma, Daphne, and Fred tried to get to the bottom of the werewolf mystery. Velma cradled the Ingolstadt werewolf book in her arm as they walked through the circus searching for Marius.

"Care to explain this?" Velma demanded when they finally found the circus owner. She waved the book in his face.

Marius stared at her blankly. "Well . . . it's a book. You see, they print words on sheets of paper, bind them together, and—"

Daphne sighed impatiently. "It's a book about the Ingolstadt werewolves!"

"And we found it in your office," Fred declared.

Marius was stumped. "And what, that makes me a werewolf? My office is usually unlocked. Anyone could have planted it in there."

Just as Velma was about to ask another question, a voice rang out across the circus. "Mr. Brancusi?"

"Over here," Marius called wearily. A thin, balding, middle-aged man with a briefcase strolled over.

"It's Phil Flaxman," the man said. "Call me Phil, everyone calls me Phil. Even my kids call me

Phil." He looked at the gang, who were still wearing their circus outfits. "Ooh! Circus folk!"

"Come into my office please, Phil. If you'll excuse me"—Marius shot Velma, Fred, and Daphne an angry look—"I have some business to discuss."

Velma gave the others a serious look. But Marius and Phil had already closed the door behind themselves, so the gang wandered back toward the big top, searching for more clues.

As they approached the main ring, they could hear that Shaggy and Scooby were back from their breakfast. They were arguing.

"What do you mean, you won't do the show tonight?" Shaggy demanded.

Scooby growled. "Rou heard me."

"Aw, c'mon, Scoob!"

"Ro." Scooby was still upset that Shaggy was getting all the credit when he was the one who'd done all the cool tricks.

Shaggy knelt down in front of Scooby and held a big box of Scooby Snacks. "Would you do the show again for a Scooby Snack?"

Scooby turned up his nose. "Ruh-ruh!"

"Would you do it for two Scooby Snacks?" Shaggy *really* wanted Scooby to do his circus tricks again that night.

"Rorget rit!"

"Fine." Shaggy stomped off.

He returned a moment later, pushing a wheelbarrow full of Scooby Snacks. "There are three hundred and forty-two pounds of Scooby Snacks here. Happy now?"

Scooby dove into the wheelbarrow and began to munch. "Reah! Happy now!" he said with a huge smile. It was easy to forget he was angry with Shaggy when he was stuffing his face with tasty treats.

As Fred, Velma, Daphne, and Shaggy watched Scooby chow down, Marius and Phil returned. "Thank you, Phil," Marius said. "We'll see you at tonight's show!"

"Wouldn't miss it!" Phil said as he waved good-bye.

"Guess what?" Marius said, his eyes

sparkling. "That man just bought out all the seats for tonight's performance. We're doing a private show for the Wûlfsmööon guy."

Shaggy gaped at Marius. "Wulfric Von Rydingsvard?! Omigosh, omigosh, omigosh!"

Fred stepped over to Shaggy and gave him a paper bag to breathe into. Marius looked concerned. "Is he going to be all right?"

Fred shrugged. "As all right as he ever is."

Velma looked up from the Ingolstadt book, which she was studying. She narrowed her eyes at Marius.

"I am not a werewolf!" Marius insisted again.

"I really don't think it's him, Velma," Fred agreed.

"We'll see." Velma kept squinting at Marius. "Okay, so I found out what a carbonado is. It's also known as a black diamond."

Shaggy suddenly screamed so violently that he popped his paper bag.

Daphne rubbed her ear. "Thanks, Shaggy. Deaf in this ear now."

"Black diamond," Shaggy screamed.

"What?" Fred yelled, covering his ears.

"Wulfric! Wulfric! Wulfric!" Shaggy hollered.

"Shaggy!" Velma shouted back, shaking him. "How about a verb?"

Shaggy calmed down for just a moment, and then he freaked out again. "Wears! Wears! Wears!"

Fred handed Shaggy another paper bag, then said, "Let's see, if we put them together . . . Wulfric . . . wears . . . black diamond?"

Shaggy pointed at Fred and nodded. Then he pointed at a Wûlfsmôóon billboard. Everyone noticed the same thing at once. Wulfric was wearing an amulet with a huge black diamond!

"Well," Velma mused, "I guess we know what the werewolves' next target is. . . ."

Fred nodded. "And this time, we'll be ready!"

CHAPTER 9

Later that night, the gang stood outside Archambault's trailer. The circus was about to start, but Archambault was nowhere to be seen. The door of his trailer dangled off its hinges, and the inside was a mess.

"I hate to say it, but it looks like the werewolf has struck again," Velma observed, her nose still in the Ingolstadt werewolf book.

Marius paced nearby. "Archambault is gone! We can't find him anywhere! And look at his trailer—there's obviously been a struggle here."

Oliverio stormed up just as Marius finished talking. He pointed at Fred. "You! Where is she?!"

"She?" Fred asked, backing away from Oliverio. The guy made him nervous.

Oliverio stepped forward menacingly. "Where is my Lena?! She is missing! You two are planning to run off together, aren't you?"

"What?" Fred asked. "No!"

Oliverio grabbed Fred by the collar. "Don't lie to me!"

Daphne realized that Oliverio was jealous—and really worried about Lena. "Oliverio, stop," she said soothingly. "Lena could have been taken by the werewolf."

"Hmph," Oliverio said. "Net Boy is the only wolf I see." He stormed off.

Marius stopped pacing long enough to look at Fred. "I hope Oliverio isn't too upset, Fred. Because you're going to be doing the trapeze with him tonight. Someone has to fill in for Lena."

Fred gulped.

"We can do this," Marius reassured them all. He began to lead the gang toward the big top. "We can! We just need to get through this show, then we can find out what happened to everyone."

As they walked up to the performance area, Velma said, "Our audience is here."

"There's Wulfric!" Shaggy exclaimed. "He looks shorter in person." Wulfric Von Rydingsvard, Phil Flaxman, and a few other people were walking toward the big top. A huge black diamond necklace hung around Wulfric's neck.

Marius looked at Wulfric, and then back at the gang. "Okay, here we go. There's just one thing you have to remember—"

Suddenly, Marius was yanked backward by a pair of huge, hairy hands.

"Marius?" Fred prompted, turning to see what he was about to say. "Yes?"

"Aw, like, not him, too!" Shaggy whimpered.

Sisko ran up, honking his horn.

Fred nodded along. "Sisko is right!" he said certainly. "The show must go on!"

"But, like, what if the werewolves show up?" Shaggy said, trying to hide.

"I'm counting on it!" Fred said. He put on Marius's top hat. "We've got a little surprise in store for them!" The lights dimmed, and Fred stepped out of the fog into a spotlight. "Ladies and gentlemen! With the finest talent from ten continents . . ."

Phil leaned toward Wulfric in the stands. "I thought there were only seven continents."

Wulfric shrugged. "Well, they're discovering new ones all the time."

Fred cleared his throat and shouted, "I present . . . the Brancusi Circus!"

The circus began, and the Mystery Inc. gang did their best to fill in for all of the missing circus performers. Daphne rode her motorcycle and took Shmatko's place in the clown act. Then Fred partnered with Oliverio on the trapeze . . . and didn't break anything. Finally, it was time for Shaggy and Scooby to come out to the center of the ring.

"Hello, Wulfric Von Rydingsvard!" Shaggy said, waving.

Wulfric had to look around before finally noticing Shaggy. "Where . . .? Oh, right." He waved.

Shaggy beamed. "I give you . . . Shaggy!" Then he lowered his voice and said, "And his performing dog."

Scooby rolled his eyes, but he began his act.

"The guy in the dog suit is fantastic!" Wulfric cried halfway through Scooby's performance.

"That's a real dog," Phil said.

Wulfric laughed. "Phil, you'll fall for anything! I bet you believe in kangaroos, too!" He was laughing so hard he didn't notice the shadowy figures creeping up behind him in the stands.

Fred looked up at Wulfric just in time to see several pairs of red eyes glowing behind the rock star's head.

"They're here!" Fred yelped. "Go!" He gestured to Velma, who pulled a rope. A sandbag swung down from above and knocked one of the werewolves away from Wulfric just as the creature reached for the musician's necklace.

The other werewolf, the one in Shmatko's clothes, jumped out of the way just in time. It grabbed for the amulet.

Wulfric turned just in time to spot the werewolf behind him. "Now this is what I've been waiting for!" He whooped. "Hello, wolfy, wolfy, wolfy!"

The wolf was surprised at the cheerful

greeting. It paused for a moment—just long enough for Daphne to hop on her motorcycle and gun her way toward Wulfric.

"Sorry, Shmatko!" she cried as she lassoed the werewolf with a rope. She dragged Shmatko the werewolf out of the stands and tied it to a pole. She backed away, saying, "We'll get you back to normal soon . . . if that's really you!"

That's when Daphne heard a low growl behind her. Three more werewolves were approaching her from the other side . . . and they were wearing Archambault, Lena, and Marius's clothes!

"Oh!" Daphne cried, trying to escape without startling them. "Not good. . . . Fred!" The werewolves stepped forward, and Daphne ran.

Back in the stands, the werewolf that had been hit with the sandbag was back in action. It leaped to its feet and reached for Wulfric's black diamond amulet.

"Hey, what—?" Wulfric gasped as the werewolf grabbed at his neck. Phil jumped on the werewolf's back and tried to pull it off of Wulfric.

"*Ow!*" Wulfric cried, trying to free himself

from the werewolf's grasp. "That's a titanium chain!"

Finally, the clasp snapped, and Wulfric's amulet came free. The werewolf shrugged Phil off its back and ran.

Just then, the werewolf wearing Lena's clothes spotted Fred and crept toward him. "Good dog . . . *goooood* doggy . . . don't bite Freddy now . . ." Fred cooed.

Oliverio leapt in front of Fred. "Come back to me, Lena! I don't care if you're a dog! Bite me and we shall stalk the night together, two wolves in love!"

The werewolf studied Oliverio, and then threw him into a wall.

"You two obviously have some stuff to work out, so I'll just be . . ." Fred said, backing away.

The Marius and Archambault werewolves were chasing Velma, Shaggy, and Scooby around the main ring. It was complete chaos in the circus—there were almost as many werewolves as there were people. Everyone ran and scattered, but the werewolves pursued them.

"I'm coming, Scoob!" Shaggy cried, as a werewolf grabbed at Scooby-Doo. He grabbed the werewolf by the arm. "Like, leave my friend alone!"

Shaggy pulled and pulled at the werewolf's arm, until finally a chunk of brown fur came off in his hand. Under the brown fur, Shaggy noticed something strange. "Red fur?" he wondered aloud.

The werewolf roared and snarled, pulling Shaggy out of his confused trance. "Zoinks!" Shaggy dropped the fur and zoomed away.

The werewolves ran after Shaggy. Soon they had Fred, Daphne, Velma, and Shaggy cornered. They were getting closer by the second.

Scooby stopped long enough to notice the fur Shaggy had dropped. "Rhut?" He thought for a moment, and then peeked out of an opening in the circus tent. He saw the animal cages, and noticed that the baboon cage was empty. His eyes grew wide as he realized something. "Rhey're rone!"

CHAPTER
10

Scooby ran to where the werewolves had the others cornered. "Raggy!" He yelled. "Rhey're raboons!"

"Raboons?" Shaggy asked. Then he looked at the werewolf in Marius's clothing and, again, at its red fur. "Baboons! Oh, man . . . What was that command Doubleday used . . . ?" Shaggy ducked as one of the werewolves slashed at him. *"Domingo!"* he cried.

The werewolf lunged again. *"Dossantos?"* Shaggy tried. "Um . . . uh . . . *descanso!*"

It was like magic. Instantly, the werewolf stopped in its tracks and stood still. All the other werewolves stood still, too . . . except for one. That werewolf turned and ran, as Shaggy explained, "They're the trained baboons! Which means Doubleday must be behind this!"

The werewolf kept running. Fred yelled, "Stop him!"

Velma looked around and noticed the cannon. "Oh, no. . . ." she muttered. But she knew what she had to do. She ran to the cannon, climbed in, and yelled, "Fred! Fire!"

Fred looked uncertain. "Are you sure?"

Velma closed her eyes. "Do it!"

Fred pulled the lever on the cannon. Velma shot out, hit the center of the trapeze net, bounced, and landed right on the escaping werewolf!

"Way to go, Velma!" Daphne cheered.

"Oh, yeah," Wulfric agreed from his seat in the stands. "Best Human Comet ever!"

As everyone hurried over, Velma pulled off the trapped werewolf's mask. It was Doubleday!

"Ow!" Doubleday yelped. "That was glued on, you know."

"It's Doubleday, all right," Velma noted.

Doubleday leaped to his feet and grabbed a

pole from the center of the circus ring. He pointed it at everyone, growling, "Get back! You won't take us that eas—"

Suddenly, there was a muffled shot. Doubleday yelped and reached around to pull a tranquilizer dart out of his backside. Then he swooned and swayed, about to fall over.

Everyone looked to see what had happened . . . and there was Archambault, standing in the shadows at the side of the circus. He was holding up a tranquilizer gun. Loose ropes hung from his arms.

"What did you do?" Fred asked.

"Is okay," Archambault said, stepping out of the shadows. He caught Doubleday as he fell to the ground and lowered the animal trainer slowly to the ground. "Just tranquilizer gun. Doubleday keep around in case of problem with animals."

"What are those ropes?" Velma asked, pointing at the ropes that hung off Archambault's arms. They looked like they'd been cut.

"Archambault tied up. But Archambault break ropes! Such thick ropes. It take hours."

Daphne stared at him. "Where were you?"

Archambault pointed to the exit. "In storage shed, back there. Come with me." He led the gang to a storage shed on the outer edge of the circus.

The gang peered inside and saw Marius, bound and gagged in a corner.

"Are you okay?" Fred asked, untying him.

"Who did this?" Marius demanded. "Did you catch him? What's going on?"

"It was Doubleday," Fred said. He turned to help Velma and Daphne free Shmatko and Lena, who were tied up nearby.

"We've already called the police," Velma said. She barely got Lena's ropes untied before they heard a loud squeal.

Oliverio ran over to embrace Lena. *"Carino!"*

"Liebling!" Lena cried.

Shmatko pulled the rest of his ropes away and stormed off. The gang followed Marius and Archambault back into the big top, just in time to see Doubleday getting carted away on an ambulance gurney.

Wulfric wandered up to see what was going

on. "Where did my amulet go?"

"I've got men searching for it, and all the other stolen jewels," said a police detective, joining the group. "But if we don't find them, we can get the information from Doubleday when he comes to. This is strong stuff, though. He could be out for hours . . . days even."

"My circus is supposed to be in Philadelphia tomorrow," Marius said. "Will that be a problem?"

"No," the detective said. "If we need you, we'll contact you."

Wulfric turned his attention to Scooby as the detective finished up his business with Marius. "You were the best thing in the show, my friend. And that dog costume is brilliant."

Scooby shook his head. "Rog rostume?"

The next morning, the gang joined Marius and the rest of the circus performers as they boarded the train for Philadelphia.

"Thanks again for all your help," Marius said. "Are you sure I can't give you anything?"

"No thanks," Fred said, waving him off. "We're just glad we could help."

Marius held up a lockbox. "We did some major box office while you were helping out . . . this thing is crammed with cash. So anytime you want to see the circus, it's on the house. And all the churros you can eat!"

"Yes!" Shaggy cheered.

Scooby just frowned. He was still upset with Shaggy for taking all the credit for his act.

"And maybe I could do the high-wire next time, huh?" Fred grinned.

Marius looked uncomfortable. "Uh, let's think about . . . whether that's . . . the best . . . uh . . . well, good-bye!" He hustled onto the train.

Archambault stopped to bid the gang good-bye. "Archambault say good-bye, also!"

Velma waved. "Good-bye, Archambault. Thanks for everything!"

"Okay! I hope they find all those jewels," he said. "Especially that black diamond. It seemed very nice, *oui*?"

As Archambault stepped up onto the train, Sisko and Shmatko approached Daphne. "Hey, Motorcycle Girl!" Shmatko said in a friendly voice. "After this little break, I finally decide clowning is not for me. So now I go to New York to pursue my true love . . . theatre!"

"That's great, Shmatko," Daphne said. "I'm sure you're going to be a huge success."

"Of course, Sisko will miss me terribly." Shmatko looked at Sisko, who honked sadly in response. "But a man has got to be doing what it is that a man has got to be doing! Good-bye!"

Daphne waved. "Good-bye!"

Sisko mimed tears as he waved good-bye to Shmatko. But the second Shmatko was out of sight, his tears cleared up. He rolled his eyes and said, "I thought he'd never leave. Cheers!" He stepped up and boarded the train.

As the train chugged off, Fred mused, "Well, another case solved."

"I don't know," Velma sighed. "Something's still bugging me."

Daphne nodded. "Yeah, I miss the part where the bad guy says he would've gotten away with it, if it hadn't been for us."

"Wait!" Velma cried, raising her finger into the air. "Archambault said 'black diamond.' But the last he heard that gem was a 'carbonado.'"

"So?" Fred asked.

"And do you remember what Doubleday said when we unmasked him? He said, 'You won't take *us* that easily.' He said *us*! Like he had a partner in crime! And Archambault caught Doubleday after he tranquilized him. He could have grabbed the black diamond!" Velma looked around, nodding as the others began to get it. "And Archambault said he broke his ropes, but that rope hadn't been broken. The ends looked like they'd been cut!"

"And the book!" she cried. "Archambault was the one who knocked the Ingolstadt werewolf book off the shelf. I'll bet he planted it in there!" She beamed. "Archambault was in on it!"

They all looked at the train, which was speeding away from them. "We've got to catch that train!" Velma cried.

CHAPTER
11

The Mystery Machine sped down the highway. Scooby looked out of the van's window as the Mystery Machine pulled up alongside the train. Through a window, he could see Archambault and Marius fighting. "Ruh-roh!" he barked. "Look!"

"We gotta get on that train somehow!" Shaggy said in a moment of temporary insanity. The others looked at him curiously. "What?" he asked nervously. "What are you looking at?"

Fred smiled. "Shaggy . . . how far can you jump?"

"Huh?" Shaggy's eyes widened as he realized what Fred was suggesting. "Oh, no. Oh, no no"

A few minutes later, Shaggy and Scooby were on the roof of the Mystery Machine, staring at the speeding train zooming along beside them.

"Come on, guys," Daphne urged. "Jump, so I can get up there."

Shaggy moaned. "Like, how did we get talked into this, Scoob?"

Scooby turned away. He was still mad at Shaggy. *"Hmph!"*

"How can you still be mad? I said I was sorry!"

Daphne was getting annoyed. She grabbed a clown horn from the floor of the van and honked it loudly. Startled, Shaggy and Scooby jumped off the roof and onto the top of the train.

A moment later, the road began to curve away from the train tracks, making it impossible for anyone else to jump onto the train.

"I guess it's just us, Scoob," Shaggy said, looking mournfully at the van. He followed along as Scooby ran toward the front of the train. They stopped and leaned down over to peek in a window.

Inside, Archambault and Marius were still fighting. Archambault had Marius pressed up against a wall and held him off his feet with just one hand. He shook the lockbox in Marius's face. "Tell Archambault where is key, or Archambault get angry!" he screamed.

"We gotta stop him!" Shaggy shouted.

Scooby looked away, upset. "Re?"

Shaggy sighed impatiently. "Scoob, I'm sorry. I know it was wrong to treat you like a trained animal. I was a complete—" He broke off as he thought of something.

Scooby thought of the same thing at the same moment. "Rained animals!"

They ran like crazy toward the animal car on the train.

"Hey . . . animals!" Shaggy called. "We need your help!"

The animals all stared at him blankly.

"Uh . . . *escuchenme*! *Por favor . . . uh . . . ayudame . . .*"

Scooby held up one hand to stop him. "Rallow me." He sauntered over to the baboon cage and started barking at them. The baboons listened intently, and then began to nod.

"Scooby speaks baboon?" Shaggy mused. "Who knew?" He took a ring of keys from a hook on the wall and began to unlock the cage with the horses in it. Once everything was ready, he and Scooby made their way back to Marius's car.

Inside, Archambault had Marius tied up like a prisoner. He was hastily dumping the contents of the lockbox—including the jewels—into a sack.

That's when Scooby rode into the car on horseback, playing a bugle!

Archambault stared at Scooby, stunned. Then he began to laugh. "Archambault never punch a horse before," he said. "Could be fun!"

Just as he reeled back to charge at Scooby's horse, the baboons ran into the room. Archambault dropped the sack with the jewels, reached behind his back, and grabbed for his tranquilizer gun. "Sleepy time for the monkeys!"

The gun clicked uselessly. Archambault stared at it. "What?! Where are the darts?" He looked around and saw Shaggy, who had climbed in through the window behind Archambault.

Shaggy grinned, and picked up the sack of loot. "Don't worry. I've got the darts right here." He patted at his pocket.

Archambault lunged at Shaggy, but the baboons pounced on him.

"No!" Archambault cried. "Bad monkeys!"

Scooby and Shaggy took the chance to slip out of the train window while Archambault was occupied. "Like, what do we do now?"

"Hello, peoples!" Suddenly, Archambault's head popped up over the edge of the roof.

Scooby's eyes widened. "Run!"

Archambault chased after them, yelling, "Come back here, dog and hippie! Archambault won't hurt you . . . much!"

Shaggy glanced at Scooby. "Did he just call me a hippie?"

They kept running, with Archambault getting closer by the second.

Shaggy and Scooby yelped as the train approached a bunch of low-hanging tree branches. They swerved, but Archambault just let the trees hit him. He puffed out his chest and let the thick tree limbs smash against his rock-hard body. "Rikes!" Scooby said, feeling his own chest.

"Jump!" Shaggy shouted to Scooby when they reached the end of the train car. The tracks sped by at an alarming speed beneath them. Shaggy gulped nervously. He looked for Scooby, and then realized his pal had already jumped and was staring at him from the top of the next train car.

Shaggy crouched down and leaped across the gap just as Archambault reached for him. Shaggy grabbed at the top of the train car, but his body slid down. He was going to fall!

Just in time, Scooby grabbed at Shaggy's shirt collar and pulled him up to safety.

"Thanks, buddy!" Shaggy said, hugging Scooby happily.

"Ranytime, pal," Scooby said.

They only had a moment to celebrate before Archambault was after them again. "Scoob! I've got an idea! Follow me!" Shaggy cried. They ran to the end of the train car and jumped . . . but instead of making it to the other side, they both fell out of view.

Archambault leaned over the edge of the train car, wondering where they'd gone. As he did, Shaggy reached up and stuck a tranquilizer dart right in the tip of Archambault's nose!

"*Ahhh!*" he cried, reeling backward. "*Mon nez! Mon . . .*"

Shaggy and Scooby high-fived as Archambault tipped and toppled and finally crashed to the roof of the train car. "Rood rob, Raggy!"

"You, too, Scoob!"

When the train stopped, it took several police officers to drag Archambault's huge body off into a police car.

"This guy is tough!" one of the police officers said. "I think that tranquilizer is starting to wear off already. . . ."

Archambault snored in response.

Marius looked at the gang and sighed happily. "Apparently, Archambault and Doubleday were both angry when my uncle left me the circus. I understand it . . . They worked for him for years, then suddenly his nephew comes in and wants to change everything."

"Anyway," Velma said, "when Archambault saw that Doubleday was caught, he double-crossed him, hoping to make off with the jewels *and* the box-office money."

The police officers were still trying to wrestle Archambault into the police car when he opened his eyes to say, "And Archambault would have get away with it if it don't be for the young peoples and the nosy dog!"

Daphne smiled happily. "Ah . . . I do like to hear that."

Archambault toppled backward into the police car. As the officers drove him away, a stretch limo pulled up. Wulfric hopped out.

"Well," Fred said, "I guess that wraps it up."

"I got your call," Wulfric said. He paused. "Hey, that's a train. Toot, toot!"

Shaggy walked over to Wulfric and said, "Uh, Mr. Wulfric, sir? Um, hi. We caught Doubleday's accomplice and, uh . . . he had this in his pocket." He held up Wulfric's amulet.

"Brilliant! Just brilliant!" Wulfric gazed at his black diamond amulet happily as Phil stepped out of the car with a big case. Phil opened the case to reveal six identical amulets and one empty space inside. "That one's my second favorite!" Wulfric grinned. "Hey, I really gotta thank you. Is there anything I can do for you?"

Marius nodded. "I have to thank them again! They won't take money, though—I tried."

Wulfric nodded. "Well, there must be something, right?"

Shaggy thought for a second before saying, "Hmm . . . maybe there is . . ."

Late that night, Shaggy and Scooby sat in fancy theater seats and munched happily on churros, relaxing after their big day. "This is the best!" Shaggy cheered. "Right, buddy?"

"You said it, *amigo*!" Scooby grinned.

The lights dimmed, and Wûlfsmööon appeared on the stage in front of them. "Hello, you guys! Are you ready to rock?"

Scooby and the gang all shouted, "YES!"

Wulfric launched into his first song:

"Mysteries, Inc! Mysteries, Inc!
They helped me out a lot, I think!
There's a dog named Scooby and some other
* guys . . .*
and I said I'd write 'em a song but I forgot to!"

He broke off and began to scream and play his guitar.

Shaggy pumped his fist in the air, whooping.

Scooby jumped up on stage and grabbed the mic. Everyone cheered as Scooby howled, *"Scooby-Dooby-Doooooooo!"*